Treasure Twins!

Adapted by Mary Tillworth
Based on the teleplay "Ahoy, Genies!" by Lacey Dyer
Illustrated by Cartobaleno

A GOLDEN BOOK • NEW YORK

T#: 4433547
randomhousekids.com
ISBN 978-0-399-55792-7
Printed in the United States of America
10 9 8 7 6 5 4 3

It was a lovely beach day! Leah was collecting pretty shells and putting them in her bucket. She was going to make jewelry. Zac was looking for a spiky pink shell so he could make a sound like a horn.

"I heard if you blow into it, you can call a pirate ship!" he said.

Zac spotted the perfect shell . . . but he'd have to wrestle it away from a crab!

While Zac chased the crab, a giant wave washed away Leah's bucket!

"My treasures!" Leah gasped. "Now what am I going to make jewelry with?"

Suddenly, she had an idea—she would use a wish to find her beach treasures! She called to her genies-in-training, **Shimmer** and **Shine**.

The genies arrived with their pets, Tala and Nahal. "If we'd known we were going to the beach," said Shine, "we would've worn our swimsuits, too!" But with two claps, the genies were in their bathing suits.

"For my first wish," Leah said, "I wish I could find more beach treasures!"

Shine clapped her hands again.
"Boom, Zahramay! First wish of the day!"

"Is this a . . . treasure map?" asked Leah.
Shine beamed. "Yup! A map to beach treasures!"
"But I was hoping the treasures would just appear," said Leah.
Shine smiled sheepishly. "Sorry, Leah."

"It's okay," Leah said. "Sometimes mistakes happen. At least with this one, we get to go on a treasure hunt!" Leah and the genies followed the map into a cave.

It was very dark in the cave. Shine clanged her bracelets together and the crystals on the walls twinkled with light! Leah read the first clue. "'Watch the step down below. Through a tunnel you will go.'" She frowned. "But all I see are these giant crystals."

Just then, the floor opened,
and Leah and the genies slid

DOWNNN!

"Looks like we found
the tunnel!" laughed Shine.

The girls landed with a thump . . . across from a giant ship!

Shimmer gasped. "Oh my genie, a pirate ship!"

"The same ship as the one on the map," said Leah. "Let's swim over!"

Shimmer dipped a toe into the water and shivered.
"Swimming's out, unless we want to turn into icicles."
Shine spotted Tala monkeying around on a vine.
"We can swing across on these vines!"

Leah and the genies
swung from vine to vine until they
reached the pirate ship.

With a poof of magic, Shimmer and Shine
made pirate outfits appear on everyone. Now
they were ready to hunt for pirate treasure!

Leah read the next clue. "'Set your sail, point it west. Then you'll find your treasure chest.'"

"Let's get moving!" cheered Shine.

"Okay," said Leah. "For my second wish, I wish this ship would move!"

Shimmer clapped her hands. *"Boom, Zahramay! Second wish of the day!"*

A gust of wind filled the sails—and blew the treasure map into the water!

Shimmer shook her head. "Looks like I made the wind a little *too* windy."

"It's okay. You tried really hard, and you did get us moving," said Leah.

With a bit of fancy steering, the friends got the map back.

Leah tried to read the next clue, but
the water had smudged the map!
"I wish someone would just tell us
where the treasure is," sighed Leah.

"*Shimmer and Shine, someone tell us divine!*" chanted Shine.
A loud squawk filled the air. It was a pirate's parrot!
"He's here to tell us where the treasures are!" said Shine.
Shimmer walked toward some vines. "Maybe it's this way."
"Cold!" shouted the parrot.

Leah turned toward a large rock.
"Hot!" squawked the parrot.
Leah realized something. "He's playing
the hot-and-cold game. When we're close
to the treasure, he'll say 'Hot!' But when
we're far away, he'll say 'Cold!'"

"Hot! Hot! Hot!"

squawked the parrot as Leah approached the rock.

The friends lifted the rock and
found a chest filled with riches!
"Look at all these treasures!"
exclaimed Leah. "I can't believe
we found them!"

Leah and the genies headed back to the
beach to make jewelry with their beach treasures.

Leah gave Shimmer and Shine two sparkly
necklaces. "These are for my favorite genies!"
"Thanks, Leah," said Shimmer. "We'll treasure
our treasures forever!"

Just then, $\mathbb{Z}a\mathbb{c}$ returned. The genies and their pets quickly hid behind a sand castle so he wouldn't see them.

Leah grabbed a pink shell and handed it to him. "I don't know if it'll call a pirate ship . . . but give it a try."

Zac took a deep breath and blew. *Toot!*

The pirate ship appeared—with a little magical help from Shine.

Zac ran to check it out. "Holy horsefeathers—a pirate ship!"

Leah giggled when the two sand-covered genies popped out from behind the sand castle.

"It's a good thing we made mistakes—or we wouldn't have gone on a treasure hunt!" said Leah.

"And you wouldn't have made us these!" said Shimmer, touching her necklace.

"Exactly!" Leah said. "We fixed our mistakes, and the day turned out great!"